LARK and the
DESSERT DISASTER

NATASHA DEEN

Illustrated by MARCUS CUTLER

orca Echoes

ORCA BOOK PUBLISHERS

Library and Archives Canada Cataloguing in Publication

Deen, Natasha, author
Lark and the dessert disaster / Natasha Deen; illustrated by Marcus Cutler.
(Orca echoes)

Issued in print and electronic formats.
ISBN 978-1-4598-2067-8 (softcover).—ISBN 978-1-4598-2068-5 (PDF).—
ISBN 978-1-4598-2069-2 (EPUB)

I. Cutler, Marcus, illustrator   II. Title.   III. Series: Orca echoes

PS8607.E444L3328 2019   jc813'.6   c2018-904771-2
c2018-904772-0

Simultaneously published in Canada and the United States in 2019
Library of Congress Control Number: 2018954160

Summary: In this illustrated early chapter book, Lark and Connor Ba have been invited to
judge a community baking contest. But when a contestant's dessert is sabotaged, the amateur
detectives have to solve the case if they are going to have any sweets left to sample.

Orca Book Publishers gratefully acknowledges the support for its publishing
programs provided by the following agencies: the Government of Canada,
the Canada Council for the Arts and the Province of British Columbia through
the BC Arts Council and the Book Publishing Tax Credit.

Edited by Liz Kemp
Cover artwork and interior illustrations by Marcus Cutler
Author photo by Richard Jervis

ORCA BOOK PUBLISHERS
orcabook.com

Printed and bound in Canada.

22 21 20 19 • 4 3 2 1

For Mom and Dad
—ND

Chapter One

My name is Lark Ba, and I was cooling my heels. Well, not really. My heels weren't hot. "Cool your heels" is something my *halmoni*—that's Korean for "grandmother"—says when I'm really excited to do something, but I have to be patient-like and wait. Right now I was waiting for my mom and dad to finish getting ready. I was cooling my heels with my dog, Max. We sat next to my little brother, Connor. He wasn't cooling his heels like me and Max though. He was studying. Connor was reading a book about baking.

"Did you know North Americans eat two billion cookies every year?" he asked.

"That's a lot of cookies," I said.

"This book says it works out to three hundred cookies a person." Connor closed his book and looked at me serious-like. "Do you know what that means?"

"Someone has been eating our cookies," I said, "because there's no way Mom and Dad let us have three hundred cookies a year."

"Do you think they eat our share when we're sleeping?"

"That would explain why they're always so strict about bedtime," I said.

"And why they don't like us getting out of bed and going to the kitchen to get a glass of water," added Connor.

"We'll have to do some—" I tried to think of the word. It started with a *k* or an *o*, and it was a *great* word that meant "secret." I couldn't think of it, so I said, "Secret investigating. If we put our heads together, we can solve this mystery."

He made a frowny face. "Can we be our own clients?"

That summer Connor and I had become private investigators. We'd found the missing key to the library for Mrs. Robinson, recovered stolen diamond earrings for the Lees and discovered who had been playing pranks at the community theater.

Being a P.I. is a lot of fun! I like figuring out puzzles and putting clues together, and helping people solve their problems. Plus, we have a mascot. It's an alligator, because I love them. Pluser, alligator rhymes with investigator. And I really like that!

"I think we can be our own clients," I said. "But our case will have to wait. We have a more important job today."

"You mean going to the baking contest," said Connor. "And making sure we eat as many cookies and cakes as we can. I have to get in those three hundred cookies before Mom and Dad catch us."

"No—well, yes, that's true. But we're also judges for the contest, so we need to make sure we're fair about who we choose to win." Judging the contest was a ~~privillage~~ ~~privaledge~~ privilege we were given for being so good at solving mysteries.

Every year Mrs. Hamilton runs a baking contest. She owns a great bakery in our neighborhood called Cake'n'Bake. The winner of her contest will have their dessert sold in her bakery for four months!

Connor pulled out the paper that listed all the rules for judging. He covered up the lines so I could only see one at a time.

I have dyslexia. That means I reverse letters and numbers, and sometimes they jump around. Seeing only one line at a time helps the words stay still. "We have to judge the best dessert. That means tasting the food—"

"That'll be easy," said Connor. "Nothing burned wins!"

Connor moved his hands so I could read the next line. "And we have to judge the dessert based on the presentation."

I frowned. "What do you think that means?"

"It means the cookies and cakes have to look nice when they're on the plate," he said. He pointed to the last line. "Also, we're not supposed to play favorites."

"That's going to be difficult," I said, "because I know everyone in the contest, and they're all my favorites."

"Mine too," agreed Connor.

"I wonder what kinds of treats everyone will be baking," I said.

"I heard Mr. O'Reilly is making a baked Alaska. I wonder what that is."

"Let me check." When Connor and I found out we were going to be judges, we went to the library and borrowed a whole bunch of books on baking. I thought if we know the recipes that make up the treats, it might help when it comes to judging them. I took out one of the books and looked up *baked Alaska*. "Crickets! It looks really complicated."

Connor leaned over my shoulder. "Holy smokes. They bake ice cream in an oven?"

I nodded. "Yeah, but it doesn't melt."

"That's amazing." Connor took the book from me. He flipped through the pages. "Man, I hope the contestants make some of these desserts. Look at all this—checkerboard cakes and pinwheel cookies. They look delicious!"

I nodded. "They're making me hungry, and I just ate!"

"Do you think anyone will make mandazi?"

Mandazi is one of our *babu*'s—babu is Swahili for "grandfather"—favorite desserts. They are coconut donuts, and they are delicious! "I hope so!"

"Hey." Connor frowned as he read one of the pages. "What's cream of tartar? Is that like tartar sauce? Doesn't seem like it would be very good in desserts."

"Hmm, let's check. I bet we have some in the baking cupboard."

"I don't know if that's a good idea—"

But I was already walking to the kitchen. Max ran beside me. I was too excited to get the stepladder out, so I climbed onto the counter and opened the cupboard door. "There's so much stuff in here. Hold on." I dug around and tried to be careful, but my fingers were too excited. And clumsy. I knocked over a bunch of containers of sugar and sprinkles. *Boom! Crash! Smash!*

Halmoni, Mom and Dad raced into the kitchen. They stared at the mess. They stared at Max, who was covered in sugar and sprinkles.

"Well," said Dad, "we always say Max is the sweetest dog. Lark just proved it."

After I cleaned up the mess I made, we left for the community center. On the way, I saw Mr. Herald delivering the afternoon paper. He waved. "Hello, Ba family! Lark, Connor, your picture made the afternoon edition. Good luck judging the baking contest!"

"Thank you!" I waved back.

"You have a big job ahead of you," Dad said. "You have to be fair and choose the best baking. That means only one person can win, and that might be difficult, because the others will be disappointed."

"I know," said Connor.

"Are you okay with that?" Dad asked me. "I heard Sophie is entering. Isn't she your friend, Lark?"

Sophie is my best friend. She just doesn't know it yet. "Yes, but she will understand if someone else wins."

Dad nodded. "Okay, if you're sure."

I thought about what he'd said. I turned to Connor. "You know, Dad is right. You'll have to be very serious when it comes to the judging. That might be hard because you're younger than me."

"I am not!"

"Much younger."

"Twins, Lark, we're twins!"

"I'm older."

"Only by ten minutes," he grumbled.

"Still older," I said. "Are you sure you won't agree with me when it comes to the judging?"

Dad, Mom and Halmoni laughed. "The day the two of you agree on anything," said Mom, "is a day I'd like to see!"

We got to the community center, and I was beside myself with excitement. There were all kinds of great smells coming out of the open doors. Fresh bread. Chocolate-chip cookies. I saw Mrs. Hamilton standing by one of the benches. I really like her! She has purple, spiky hair and an amazing black-velvet cape. Plus, she always gives kids a free cookie on holidays.

Mrs. Hamilton walked toward us, and I did not like the look on her face, not one bit. Nope, nope, nope.

Chapter Two

"Lark and Connor, I'm so glad you're here!" she said. "Something terrible has happened!"

"What's wrong?" asked Connor.

"There's been an incident!"

Connor frowned. "What is an incident?"

Halmoni leaned close. "That's a fancy word for 'action.'"

"Oh." I turned to Mrs. Hamilton.

"What happened?"

"Someone snuck into the baking area. They destroyed one of the desserts. I'm worried the culprit might be one of the contestants," said Mrs. Hamilton. "The two of you have already solved three mysteries in the neighborhood. Can you help me? Please, Lark and Connor. We can't have someone who ruins someone else's property participating in the contest!"

Crickets! This was terrible. I was happy to help, but I wished I'd known there would be a case. I would have worn my fedora, so everyone would know we were solving a mystery.

"We can definitely help," said Connor, "and we'll do our very best to help find the culprit."

"We'll leave you to hunt for clues. The two of you need space to work," said Mom. "If you would like our help, we'll be around."

Connor and I waved goodbye to our family, then turned to Mrs. Hamilton.

"Can you tell us exactly what happened?" I asked. This was a very important question to ask. A P.I. can't solve a case until they know what's going on.

"We have fifteen people who entered the dessert contest, and our rules were simple. They had to make their desserts here, in the community-center kitchens. That way we could make sure no one would buy something from the store and pretend they'd baked it. When they arrived this morning, we checked their baking supplies and ingredients, and then they were allowed to go to the kitchens and start baking."

I nodded.

"That sounds fair," said Connor.

"Everyone had to have their dessert ready ten minutes before the contest opened, because I hired a photographer to take pictures. After that the contestants were supposed to bring their desserts to the judging stage. Then the contest would begin. Only..." Her lip trembled. "I was running around, helping folks carry their desserts to the display area, when I heard yelling coming from one of the kitchens. One of the contestants' desserts had been tossed on the floor. It's terrible!"

I agreed. "It's not nice to destroy someone else's work."

"We should talk to the person whose dessert was destroyed," said Connor. "They might have some more information for us."

"Follow me," said Mrs. Hamilton. She led us down one of the hallways. "Do you know a girl named Sophie? She's about the same age as you."

"Oh no," groaned Connor. "Don't tell me you think she did it!"

"No," said Mrs. Hamilton. "Sophie is the one whose dessert was destroyed."

Double crickets! It was bad enough that someone had had their work tossed on the floor. But it was extra bad that the person was Sophie.

We followed Mrs. Hamilton to a cheerful yellow kitchen with a very sad Sophie. She sat at one of the tables, and she had her head down on the table.

"Thank you, Mrs. Hamilton," said Connor. "We'll talk to Sophie."

"Thank you for helping," said Mrs. Hamilton. "I'm going to check on the other contestants. We've held off the judging until we can clear this up. But if we wait too long, people will get bored and leave. If you can't find out who is responsible within an hour, I won't have any choice but to let everyone participate or call off the event." She clutched her hands together. "I hate to think of someone doing a terrible thing like that and then maybe winning the contest."

"We'll do our very best," I said.

"Thank you," said Mrs. Hamilton. "If you need me, come and find me."

Connor leaned in. "I don't know if an hour is enough time."

"I don't know either," I said. "But we have to try."

I walked over to Sophie. "Hello, Sophie," I said.

She lifted her head. "Hi, Lark and Connor."

Connor blinked. "That's it?"

"Yes."

"Just *Hi, Lark and Connor*?" he asked.

"Yes," she said.

"But you usually say, *Hello, baa baa Lark sheep*," he said.

"Oh," she said. "I do?"

"Yes," he continued. "Then I get mad, because I think you're being mean."

"And I try to explain you're just joking because our last name is Ba, and *baa* is the sound sheep make," Lark said.

"Oh," said Sophie. "I guess I'm too upset to make jokes or be mean."

"Okay, can you tell us about your day?" asked Connor.

I smiled at my brother. It was a great detective question.

Her eyes got watery. "I made kutia. It's a wheat berry pudding, and it takes a really long time to make. You have to soak the berries overnight. The next day, you have to boil them with other ingredients like milk. It has to boil for four hours. And you have to be careful because it's really easy to burn milk."

"It sounds like a lot of work," I said.

"It is. But I was happy to do it because my *babushka* is visiting, and I knew she would be so proud of me for trying. There's so much stirring and baking to kutia. But I did it, and it looked so good! And it tasted even better." She wiped away her tears, then pointed at the floor. "Now look. My dessert is nothing but a cloudy patch on the floor. I cleaned up the rest of it and put it in the garbage."

"How did it go from being all ready to being on the floor?" asked Connor.

"I went to ask Mrs. Hamilton for permission to bring my babushka into the kitchen. Only contestants are allowed in the baking area, to make sure no one cheats. But I thought it might be okay."

"It's always good to ask," I said.

She nodded.

"I wanted my babushka to take some pictures of my special dessert. Mrs. Hamilton said it was against the rules to have anyone but the bakers in the back area. So I went back to my kitchen. That's when I saw the kutia on the floor." She covered her face and started to cry.

Chapter Three

I got some tissues and gave them to her.
Then I gave her a hug. Seeing Sophie sad
made me sad.

"Did you see anyone else coming
out of the kitchen?" asked Connor.

She shook her head.

"What about when you were making
the kutia? Did you notice anyone hanging
around?"

"Not really. I was so busy. I went to

the bathroom a couple of times and saw Mrs. Delaney, Mr. O'Reilly and Mrs. Lee, but that was it."

"Do you have any ideas about who might have done this?" I asked.

She shook her head again. "We all want to win, but I can't imagine anyone would do this." Sophie stood up and threw her tissues in the garbage. Then she went to the sink and washed her hands. "There's a door at the back of the kitchen. It's kind of hard to see the door, so maybe someone snuck inside?" She thought for a bit. "I didn't see anyone in the area who didn't have permission to be here, but you never know."

"We should ask around," said Connor.

"And we should look at their clothes," I said. "There might be bits of Sophie's dessert left on their clothes."

"That's a good point," agreed Connor. "If you throw pudding on the floor, some of it's sure to get on you."

At the first kitchen we found Mrs. Lee. She was making mooncakes.

"These are a real Chinese delicacy. Traditionally, they're made during the mid-autumn festival, when we celebrate the moon," she said. She smoothed her hands on her apron.

I took a good look at her apron. It was clean. No sign of splattered kutia.

"They are given to friends and family to bring good luck." She winked. "What better dessert to make than one that brings good luck to the people you love."

"They look delicious," I said. "And very pretty." They did. Mrs. Lee's mooncakes were round and golden, with imprints of lotus flowers on top.

"I put a salted egg yoke in the middle of each cake to symbolize the full moon," she said, "but you didn't come here to talk about my dessert. You're here because someone ruined Sophie's lovely kutia."

I nodded. "Did you notice anything strange?"

"Or maybe you can think of a contestant who would've wanted to ruin

Sophie's chances of winning?" asked Connor.

"Hmm," she said. "When everyone found out Sophie was making kutia, we all figured she was a shoo-in to win."

Connor frowned. "What do shoes have to do with winning?" he whispered.

I shook my head and looked at Sophie's rainbow-colored sneakers. "I don't know."

Mrs. Lee put her hand on Sophie's shoulder. "I can't imagine anyone would do something so unkind—no matter how badly they wanted to win. But... something did happen that I thought was strange. I saw a man coming in through the back door."

"The photographer Mrs. Hamilton hired?"

"No," said Mrs. Lee. "It was someone else. That door is supposed to be locked."

She frowned. "No one's allowed to use it. But I saw him there. He had a black bag with him. Maybe he was the one who did it."

"Did you know him?"

She shook her head. "I didn't recognize him."

Wow. That was a very interesting clue! Mrs. Lee and her husband ran the General Store, and they knew practically everyone in town! If she didn't recognize him, then it was not just an interesting clue. It was an ~~intreeging~~ ~~entreaging~~ intriguing clue! "What was he wearing?" I asked.

"Jeans and a T-shirt. He had shaggy brown hair," she said.

"He might still be around," said Sophie. "We should go look for him before he gets away!"

She was right!

We thanked Mrs. Lee and dashed outside.

"Oh no!" Connor slammed to a stop. Sophie and I stumbled to a stop behind him. "Look at this crowd! How will we ever find him in all these people?"

Chapter Four

Connor was right, which was really surprising. Who knew he could be correct about stuff?

"We'll have to look very carefully," I said. "We don't want the bad guy to know we're looking for him."

Connor nodded. "Mrs. Lee said he had a black bag, right? Let's split up and look for a guy who has a black bag like that."

Sophie and I went to the right. Connor went to the left.

We checked by the fountain. The only people there were parents with their babies.

"Maybe he's trying to get away," said Sophie. "We should check the parking lot."

"Okay," I said, "but we'll have to be careful and stay on the sidewalk."

"No duh, Lark." Sophie rolled her eyes. "Neither of us wants to get run over!"

I took a breath and decided to be patient with her because she was having a bad day.

We headed to the parking lot, but it was empty except for the cars and trucks.

"I thought we'd find him there," said Sophie sadly.

"It was a good idea," I said. "Let's keep checking." We went to the playground. I grabbed Sophie's shoulder.

"Look! Over there!" I pointed to the slide. "There's a man who fits the description! We should talk to him.

"Stay here and keep an eye on him," I said, then dashed away. When I came back, I had Halmoni with me. "I've explained everything to her. She's going to help us."

Halmoni nodded. "I'm very good at talking to grown-ups."

Together we raced over to him. I said, "Excuse me, sir?"

The man turned and gave us a confused smile. "Yes? Can I help you?"

"We're investigating an incident at the baking contest. Do you know anything about it?" I said.

Halmoni leaned in. "That's a great question," she whispered to me and Sophie, "but he might not know about the contest. He might be a parent or uncle who came to the park with his child."

"That's a good point," said Sophie. She glared at the man. "Who are you, and why are you here?"

He jumped back in surprise.

"Are you part of the contest?" Halmoni asked politely. "This is Sophie"—she put her hand on Sophie's shoulder—"and she's one of the bakers. And Lark"—she put her other hand on my shoulder—"is one of the judges."

"Oh," he said. "I'm one of the photographers."

"*One* of the photographers? How many of you are here?" asked Halmoni.

He smiled. "Mrs. Hamilton hired a photographer to take pictures for her bakery. And the mayor hired me to take pictures for the town's website." He stopped smiling and looked concerned. "What was the incident? What happened?"

"Someone destroyed my dessert," said Sophie. "Was it you?"

His eyes went wide. "Me? No! I would never do something like that!"

"Prove it," said Sophie. "You match the description of the guy who was lurking around the kitchen area."

"When did the accident—"

"It wasn't an accident," I said. "Someone did it on purpose."

"When did it happen?" he asked.

"About thirty minutes ago," said Sophie.

"That wasn't me," he said. "I wasn't there thirty minutes ago."

"Is there any way you can prove that?" I asked in my nicest voice.

"Actually, I can." He reached into his bag and pulled out a video camera. "Look at this. I was here at the playground, filming, when your dessert was destroyed." He hit the Play button, and a video of kids running around started up on the screen. "See? The kids and their parents came up and talked to me. I asked them about their favorite desserts and what they were most looking forward to eating. So that proves I didn't just set up the camera and walk away."

He put the video on fast-forward, and we watched it to make sure he was telling the truth. In some of the shots, I could see him. Plus, there was a clock,

so we knew the time. He wasn't the one who destroyed Sophie's dessert.

"Thank you," I said.

"You're welcome." He turned to Sophie. "I'm sorry someone did that to you."

"Did you film any other place?" I asked. "Maybe your video got a shot of the building."

He frowned. "I can check and see," he said. "I've been filming all morning, so it's a lot of video to go through. It might take a while, but I'll do it now and come find you when I'm done."

I held out my hand, and he shook it. "Thank you for your help," I said. "My little brother—"

"Twin brother," Sophie corrected me.

"—*twin* brother is Connor. He looks kind of like me, and he's wearing a blue shirt. If you see him, you can tell him too."

"Okay, my name is Ismet. I hope you find your guy," he said. "Thanks for letting me help. I've never been part of an investigation before!"

Chapter Five

"We should check the judging stage," I said.

Sophie stopped, and her eyes got wet. "I'd like to see the other desserts, but it's going to make me too sad. You better go without me."

"Are you okay to be by yourself?"

She nodded. "I'll wait by the doors."

Halmoni and I were walking to the judging stage when Connor came running up to us.

Sophie must have seen him too, because she raced to us. "Did you find him?"

"I found a man who fits the description," he said. "He came into the building, but I lost him. He's around here somewhere."

"Let's go find him," I said.

"I'm going to go that way." Sophie pointed left. "You guys go the other way."

"Agreed." We looked and looked.

Connor pointed. "There he is!"

"Sir! Sir!" I waved and waved.

The man looked up and waved back. "My name is Jun."

We ran over to him.

"Can I take a photo of you?" he asked. "Mrs. Hamilton hired me to take pictures of today's event for her website and social media."

"That would be lovely," said Halmoni. "I am Halmoni. And these are today's judges, Lark and Connor."

Jun took a couple of pictures, and then Sophie joined us. "Hello, Jun. Thank you for taking the pictures of me and the kutia. At least I'll have the photo."

"I heard about what happened," he said. "I'm sorry your beautiful dessert was destroyed."

Sophie's eyes got watery. "Thank you." She blinked and walked away.

"We were wondering if you could help us with the investigation," said Connor. "Someone matching your description was seen in the baking area."

"Oh." He nodded. "That was me."

Wow. I couldn't believe he was already confessing!

"Mrs. Hamilton wanted photos of the bakers and their desserts for her website," he continued. "I had permission to be there." He looked over to where Sophie sat. She was in the corner with her head all droopy, looking sad. "I promise I didn't do anything to ruin her dessert. That was a mean thing to do."

I believed him. I looked over at Connor. He looked like he believed Jun too.

"Hmm," I said. "Did you notice anyone acting strangely?"

He laughed. "Everyone was working hard and worrying about the time. They were anxious, but not strange!"

"So you didn't see anything that seemed out of the ordinary?" asked Connor.

"No," he said. "Everything seemed normal."

Connor spoke again. "Or maybe someone who was there who didn't have permission to be there?"

Jun thought for a bit. He looked into the distance. "I was taking pictures and asking the contestants questions. Some of them were there. Some of them weren't around—they were in the display area or they were in the other kitchens, talking to their fellow bakers."

"Do you remember any of the people who weren't in their kitchens?" I asked.

"I'm sorry, I don't. Not every contestant agreed to have me take a photo of them or their dessert. Some people don't like any distractions when they're working."

"How did you know which ones were okay to have their picture taken?"

"Mrs. Hamilton had camera stickers made. If contestants didn't mind having me around, they put a sticker with their name on it on the counter. That's how I knew."

"One of our witnesses said they saw you using the back exit, and no one was supposed to do that," said Connor.

Jun nodded. "Yes, it's true. The door wasn't supposed to be open during the contest. I needed some extra equipment. When I saw the door was already open, I thought it was okay to use it. The door was a shortcut to the parking lot. I didn't see anyone when I went outside though. So if the person used that door, they must have run outside and kept going. I didn't see anyone in the parking lot or getting into a car."

"Okay," I said. "Thank you for your help."

"Do you want to go through the pictures I took?" asked Jun. "Maybe you'll see something."

"That would be very helpful," I said. "Thank you."

We scrolled through his camera roll. There were pictures of Sophie at the stove, stirring her kutia, Mrs. Lee with flour on her nose, Mr. Barker pretending to eat a lemon. We saw Mrs. Delaney, holding up a big bag of chocolate chips and smiling. There were our two friends, Kate and Franklin, holding up a tray of Nanaimo bars.

"Do you see anything in the background of the photos that might be helpful?" Connor asked. "Because I don't."

I sighed. "No. I don't think so."

"I'm sorry I couldn't be more helpful," said Jun.

"It's not your fault," said Connor. "Thank you anyway."

Chapter Six

"Maybe we'll see something helpful in the judging area," I said. "Let's go check."

The desserts for the contest were amazing! Mrs. Robinson had made a cake that looked like a tree, with green icing for the leaves and little candies for the grass and stones. Miss Balza had made sugar cookies that were the faces of emojis. Mrs. Delaney had made a sunshine cake, a lovely yellow cake with white frosting. Everything looked so delicious! I hoped we could solve the case soon, because I was getting really hungry!

"Hello, Lark and Connor," said Miss Balza as she came up to Connor, Halmoni and me. "I heard you were on another case."

"Yes," said Connor, "we are, but we're not having any luck."

I looked around. "Did you see Sophie? She was with us a minute ago, but she's disappeared. I thought maybe she came here to look at the desserts."

Miss Balza shook her head and made her curly red hair bounce. "No, I haven't seen her. It's very sad about her dessert. I thought she was a shoo-in to win."

There it was again, a mention of Sophie's shoes. After we solved this case, I was definitely going to find out what made them special.

"That's the motive," said Connor. "Someone wanted to get rid of her dessert so she didn't win." He frowned. "Did you notice Miss Balza mentioned Sophie's shoes?" Connor whispered.

I nodded. "That's the second time someone's talked about them."

"Those shoes must be an important clue. I wonder why the dessert destroyer didn't do something with them."

"Probably because she was wearing her shoes," I said.

He nodded. "That's a good point." He tapped his chin. "I wonder if the culprit threw the dessert on the floor for that reason? Maybe they thought Sophie wouldn't want to get kutia all over her shoes and would take them off."

"Then the culprit would steal them," I said. "That's good thinking, Connor. Let's keep that in mind."

"It's very cruel, what that person

did to her dessert," said Mrs. Robinson as she came up to us. "Sophie worked very hard on it, and she deserved to have it in the contest."

"We're trying very hard to figure out who did it," I said. "Did you hear or see anything unusual?"

Mrs. Robinson and Miss Balza stopped and thought. And thought. And thought.

That was a lot of thinking!

But then both of them said, "No, I'm sorry."

"What's going on?" Mrs. Delaney had come up to us. "Are you talking about Sophie's kutia?"

"Yes," I said.

"It's a terrible thing. I heard all about it," said Mrs. Delaney.

"When Sophie was yelling and upset, maybe you came to check? Maybe you saw someone at the back door?"

"Definitely not," said Mrs. Delaney. "I was in my kitchen, working on my dessert. I never left. I heard the yelling, but then I heard Mrs. Hamilton's voice, so I knew everything would be okay."

"Okay," said Connor, trying to hide his disappointment. "Thank you." He turned to me. "We should try to find Sophie and check on her."

I agreed.

"It's kind of weird to see Sophie sad," he said. "Usually she's so annoying."

"I know, but this was a bad thing that happened. We have to make sure we try to make her feel better. We should try to as— swe—" I couldn't remember the word, but it was a good one. Halmoni used it once, and I liked the way it sounded. It started with an *a* or an *s*, and it meant "to make someone feel better."

We looked for Sophie in her kitchen. The baking dishes had been cleaned up. So had the cloudy spot on the floor. There was nothing in the room, including Sophie. We looked for her in the hallway. It was empty, except for a paper cupcake holder on the floor. I picked it up. Still no Sophie.

"Maybe she doesn't want to be found right now," said Connor.

"That could be true. Let's look at the back door. Maybe there's a clue there." I went to the back exit and pushed open the door. Sophie wasn't outside by the parking lot. I stepped back inside and threw the cupcake

holder in the compost. I noticed white icing on my fingers and wiped it off on my jeans. I hoped Mom wouldn't notice. She always says clothing is clothing and not a napkin. But we had to solve the case, and there was not enough time to find an actual napkin.

"Let's try the playground," suggested Connor.

On our way there Mrs. Delaney called us aside.

"I thought of something that might help," she said. "But before I tell you what it is, I wanted to say that I saw your picture in the afternoon edition of the paper. You two looked great!"

"Thank you," I said. "Now, do you have something that can help our case?"

"I might have a clue for you," she said. "But I didn't want to say anything in front of Mrs. Robinson or Miss Balza."

"What is it?" I asked.

"It's Mrs. Hamilton," she said. "I think she's the one who did it!"

Chapter Seven

"Mrs. Hamilton?" echoed Halmoni.

Crickets! Mrs. Hamilton? "But she's the one who organized the contest!" I said.

"Why would she want to do something like this?" asked Connor.

"I heard you talking about motive," she said. "And Mrs. Hamilton had a bunch of reasons to do it."

"Like what?"

"She was talking to Mrs. Robinson after she saw what Sophie was making. Mrs. Hamilton said she was jealous that Sophie was making kutia, because hers always burns." Mrs. Delaney leaned down close to us, and she didn't look happy at all. "I've participated every year in this contest," she said proudly. "I actually won third place a couple of times! And once I came in second!" Her happiness turned to sadness. "But the number of people who enter and come to the contest is getting smaller and smaller every year. It doesn't seem as popular as it used to be. Something sensational like a destroyed dessert will get folks talking. They might get interested in the contest again."

"That's a lot of motive!" I said.

"Man." Connor looked as miserable as Mrs. Delaney. "That's terrible. I really

like Mrs. Hamilton, and I can't believe it would be her."

"It makes me feel so down in the mouth—" said Mrs. Delaney, shaking her head.

I frowned. I didn't know what *down in the mouth* meant, but Mrs. Delaney was still talking. It would have been rude to interrupt her, so I waited.

"—but that's what I heard, and it seemed right to tell you," finished Mrs. Delaney.

Before I could ask her another question, she shook her head and walked away.

"What is *down in the mouth*?" asked Connor. "Is that a baking thing?"

"Maybe," I said. "After all, you need your mouth to chew desserts, right?"

"What do we do now?" Connor kicked at the ground. "I guess we have to talk to Mrs. Hamilton, but I feel sad, thinking she might be the one."

"I know what you mean," I said. "But feelings can make people do strange things. Remember our last case with Loi? She was so nervous about being onstage, she started hiding props so she could delay opening night."

He nodded. "Yeah, I do. But hiding stuff is a lot different than destroying someone's hard work. We should find Sophie and let her know."

I agreed.

Chapter Eight

Halmoni left us to find Mom and Dad. Connor and I looked for Sophie. We found her at the judging stage, standing by rows of cupcakes. They were iced with a whole bunch of different colors—pink, blue, red, green, orange, yellow—and sprinkled with glitter!

Connor whistled. "Wow, I think this is what unicorns would make for dessert!"

"They are beautiful," said Sophie. "Mr. Obano made them."

"I thought you didn't really want to be around the desserts," I said.

"At first I didn't," said Sophie. "But then I thought I could be sad for myself or I could go and be happy for everyone else." She shrugged. "I think I'm going to be sad for a while, so I thought I would take a break and be happy for a bit."

"That's really nice," I said, "but you might not feel happy after you hear what we have to say."

We told her about our conversation with Mrs. Delaney.

"I can't believe it," said Sophie. "She's always so nice to me!"

"We should talk to her," I said. "So far, we only have Mrs. Delaney's side.

We should listen to what Mrs. Hamilton has to say."

We went looking for Mrs. Hamilton and found her in the foyer, helping welcome all the visitors.

"Mrs. Hamilton," I said. Then I stopped and took a breath. My stomach was full of butterflies—and not in a good way. I really like Mrs. Hamilton. "We have to ask you some questions."

"Of course," she said. "Let's find a quiet spot."

When we were all seated, Sophie said, "Mrs. Hamilton, did you really say you were jealous of me for being able to make kutia?"

Mrs. Hamilton stared at us for a moment. "Yes, I did."

Sophie, Connor and I exchanged glances.

"Oh!" Mrs. Hamilton put her hand to her mouth. "Oh no! Yes, Sophie, I did say that, but I didn't throw your dessert on the floor." She took Sophie's hands in her own. "I didn't mean jealous in a bad way. I only meant that I wish I could make kutia like you. Mine never smells as good as yours does!"

"That makes me happy," said Sophie. "You're always nice to me—"

"Me too," said Connor.

"And me," I added.

"—and I'd hate to think you were just pretending and you really don't like me."

"I like all of you very much," said Mrs. Hamilton. "I wish you had been there for the conversation, Sophie. Because I am so proud of you. But I am sorry someone overheard my words and misunderstood me." She squeezed Sophie's hand. "But I'm very glad you came and talked to me about it."

"Mrs. Hamilton," I said, "you were moving around a lot today, making sure that everything was on schedule. Are you sure you didn't see anything?"

"No, I really wish I had." She checked her watch. "We only have ten minutes left. If we can't figure out who did it, then I'm going to have to make a decision. I'll have to start the contest or call it off. If I call it off, everyone will be disappointed. But if I run it, the culprit might win the prize."

Crickets! Ten minutes to solve the case? Connor and I looked at each other. I didn't know if we'd be able to do it. My best day was about to become my worstest day!

Chapter Nine

"What are we going to do?" asked Connor. "Ten minutes isn't enough time!"

"I know. I'm going to walk around," I said. "Maybe looking at the desserts will help me."

"Okay," said Connor. "I'm going to find the photographer. Jun. Maybe there's something we missed."

I walked around the displays. Then I sat in Sophie's kitchen, closed my eyes and thought. It didn't help. So I stood up and pretended to be the dessert destroyer. I checked to make sure I was alone. Then I threw a pretend kutia on the floor. I ran out of the kitchen and toward the exit. Finally I flung open the door and ran toward the parking lot.

That still didn't help. There were too many people in the kitchens and too many people outside the building. It would have been easy for the culprit to get away. It was hard to believe that someone who had made a delicious dessert could also be the person who was so ~~competative compatitive~~ competitive that they threw someone else's on the floor. I couldn't solve the case, and it made me feel grumpy and sad.

I had to go tell Connor, Sophie and Mrs. Hamilton. Not solving the case ruined my appetite. I didn't know how I was supposed to eat all those delicious treats when I felt so bad. And that made me feel even worse. Everyone had worked hard on their desserts. Mrs. Lee's mooncakes, Miss Balza's sugar cookies, Mrs. Delaney's sunshine cake.

I stopped. Frowned. Wait a minute. Mrs. Lee's mooncakes, Mr. O'Reilly's baked Alaska, Mr. Obano's colorful cupcakes, Miss Balza's emoji sugar cookies, Mrs. Delaney's sunshine cake, Mrs. Robinson's tree cake...

All of a sudden, I knew who the culprit was!

Chapter Ten

I ran to find Connor, who was running to find me.

"I know who did it!" we both said at the same time.

"Mrs. Delaney," I said.

"Right!" said Connor. "I was looking through the pictures. There was one with Mrs. Delaney holding the chocolate-chip bag. But her cake was a yellow cake with white frosting.

Plus, she was holding it in front of her apron. I think it was to cover up the splatter of the kutia when she threw it on the floor."

"Extra right," I said. "There's no chocolate in her recipe. Why would she hold it up for the photo? It doesn't make sense. Pluser, I got white icing on my hand when I opened the back door."

"Icing from the cake," he said. "She was at the back door. But when we asked her, she said she wasn't near that spot. She lied."

"Let's find Mrs. Hamilton and Sophie, and then find Mrs. Delaney!"

We went searching and found Halmoni. She helped us look for the other adults. After we had found Sophie and Mrs. Hamilton, we approached Mrs. Delaney at her dessert table.

"Hello, everyone," she said. "What's going on?"

"Mrs. Delaney," I said, "we think you're the one who destroyed Sophie's dessert."

Everyone gasped.

"I wouldn't do that!" said Mrs. Delaney. "I never went near her kitchen!"

"Why were you holding up a big bag of chocolate chips in the photo?" asked Connor. "Because you had thrown down Sophie's dessert, and your apron had the evidence. The photographers were taking pictures, so you hid the mess behind the bag."

"It's true," I said. "You didn't even use chocolate chips for your cake."

"That's not evidence," said Mrs. Delaney, scowling. "I was going to use the chocolate chips—that's why they were in the photo. Then I changed my mind." Her face got *really* scowly. "I'm allowed to change my mind."

Mrs. Delaney being grumpy was scary, but I reminded myself that there was a crime to solve. That made me feel brave. "Why was your icing on the handle of the back exit? No one's supposed to use it."

"How do you know it was my icing?" she asked.

"Because. You're the only one who made white icing," said Connor.

"Oh." She wiped her hand on the apron. "After the thing with Sophie, I went to the door to see if I could find anyone. But no one was there."

"That's not true," Mrs. Hamilton said. "Because as soon as I heard the yelling, I came running. You were still in

your kitchen." Her eyes went all squinty. "In fact, the kids asked you about that, and you said you were nowhere near the back exit."

"I came out when you weren't looking," said Mrs. Delaney. "And I checked the door. You were busy with Sophie. You didn't notice me."

Something clicked in my brain. "That's not true either," I said. "The picture of me and Connor was in the afternoon edition. Mr. Herald was delivering them when we left the house to come here. The only way you could have known about our picture is if you were outside the building. No one was allowed back here during the contest, not even Sophie's babushka. So how did you know about the photo if you were inside the entire time?"

"When I looked outside after the incident, there was a paper on the ground. I saw your photo," she said. "Anyway, if it was anyone's fault, it was Mr. Obano's. Talk to him." She looked at me. "Didn't you find his cupcake wrappers in Sophie's kitchen?"

"Yes," I said, "but you said you were never in Sophie's kitchen. So how do you know what was in it?"

Mrs. Delaney didn't say anything.

"Mrs. Delaney," said Sophie. "How could you do that? I've never done anything to you!"

"Really, how could I do that?!" Mrs. Delaney snarled at Sophie. "I've entered this contest every year! And I've never won! With fewer entrants every year, this year might be the last time it's run!"

"How could you do that? And to a child!" Mrs. Hamilton looked horrified. "Mrs. Delaney, you're an adult!"

"There are no kids or adults in a contest," she said. "Only competitors. I couldn't be sure the bake-off would happen next year—"

"I'm always going to run the contest," said Mrs. Hamilton.

"You say that now," said Mrs. Delaney. "But I couldn't be sure. And Sophie's dessert took such a long time to make. And it looked so great—I was scared she was going to win. I did what I had to do to get that prize."

"But then you lied to us," said Connor. "And you tried to blame Mrs. Hamilton."

"It was you who told the kids I was jealous!" Mrs. Hamilton gasped. "You knew I hadn't meant what I said that way!"

"Lark and Connor have already solved three cases," said Mrs. Delaney. "I couldn't risk them solving this one—not until the contest was over. Not until I'd won."

"You won't win." Mrs. Hamilton took a deep breath. "Your behavior was terrible. You destroyed someone's property, you lied to Lark and Connor, and you lied about me! Please pack up your things and leave. You are not allowed to be part of the baking contest ever again!"

Mrs. Hamilton took Mrs. Delaney by the arm. "Let's get your things and get you out of here."

"That was terrible," said Sophie. "I can't believe she wanted to win so badly that she destroyed something I made."

"Not everyone seems to understand sportsmanship," said Halmoni, "but I'm glad the three of you do!"

"I didn't even care about winning," said Sophie. "I wanted to see if I could make the dessert, and I hoped I'd make my babushka proud too."

"We are all proud of you." Halmoni put her hand on Sophie's shoulder. "I feel bad for Mrs. Delaney, because she didn't understand that sometimes you win and sometimes you lose." She bent down and looked Sophie in the eyes. "You attempted to do something you've never done before, and that's marvelous. Are you proud of yourself?"

Sophie nodded.

"Good, because that's what matters. If you try, and if you are proud of your effort, that's the important thing."

After a few minutes, Mrs. Hamilton came back. "I'm sorry for what happened," she said to Sophie, "and I know it might be difficult, but how would you feel about being a judge in the contest today?"

Sophie thought for a bit. "I don't have to agree with Lark's decision on the contest, do I?"

"No!" said Connor. "We get to choose for ourselves!"

"Good," said Sophie. "Because Lark can be...so Lark-like."

"I am not!" Wait, yes I am, and I am okay with that. "I am Lark, and I'm a very good Lark!"

"And loud," Sophie added. Then she laughed. Then she hugged me! "Thank you, Lark sheep." She grabbed Connor and pulled him into our hug.

"We solved the case just in time," I said, "because I am getting hungry!"

We started judging and everything was so delicious! And Mr. O'Reilly's baked Alaska was amazing! I picked it as my favorite. So did Connor and Sophie.

But when Mrs. Hamilton announced he'd won, he shook his head. "This bake-off was missing a contestant. We all know how hard Sophie worked on her dessert. It should have been on the stage and had a chance to win," he said. He turned to Sophie. "I'd like you to have my prize."

"That's very nice," said Sophie, "but you deserve to win."

"How about if you share it then?" Mrs. Hamilton asked. "And let's expand

the prize. So, for two months the baked Alaska will be the featured dessert at Cake'n'Bake. And for the other two months, Sophie's kutia will be the star."

Sophie grinned and nodded.

Today really was the bestest day ever!

Later there was a knock at our front door. Halmoni answered it, then called for Connor and me.

Sophie was on the porch.

"Baa baa Lark sheep," she said. "And Connor wool."

He growled. "Wool is itchy and scratchy."

"But it's warm too," she said. She held up a basket of blueberries. "I'm going to make kutia for my babushka. I wanted to know if you'd like to come and help."

We looked at Halmoni. She smiled and nodded. "If it's okay with your parents, Sophie."

"It is," she said. "What do you say?"

"I thought yesterday was a great day," I said. "But today is icing on the cake!"

Connor frowned. "Lark, there's no cake or icing. Kutia is a pudding."

"It means that even though today's a great day, sharing it with Sophie makes it even better. It makes it the bestest, most amazing kind of day."

"Oh." He nodded. "I agree. Today is icing on the cake...with sprinkles!"

THE WORDS LARK LOVES

CHAPTER ONE:

"We'll have to do some—" I tried to think of the word. It started with a k or an o, and it was a great word that meant "secret."

This great word is *covert*. For example, if you were helping to plan a surprise birthday party for your parent, you'd be doing something covert.

CHAPTER SIX:

"I know, but this was a bad thing that happened. We have to make sure we try to make her feel better. We should try to as—swe—" I couldn't remember the word, but it was a good one. Halmoni used it once, and I liked the way it sounded. It started with an a or an s, and it meant "to make someone feel better."

This is an amazingly cool word, *assuage*, and it means "to lessen." If you help a friend who is feeling sad by giving them a hug or listening to them, you help assuage their sadness.

THE WORDS LARK *ALMOST* GOT

CHAPTER THREE:

"Hmm," she said. "When everyone found out Sophie was making kutia, we all figured she was a shoo-in to win."

Connor frowned. "What do shoes have to do with winning?" he whispered.

I shook my head and looked at Sophie's rainbow-colored sneakers. "I don't know."

This word tricked Lark. She thought it was shoe-in, but the word is actually *shoo-in,* and it's another way to say someone or something is sure to win. Sophie's dessert was a shoo-in for first place, which means it was certain to win.

CHAPTER SEVEN:

"It makes me feel so down in the mouth—" said Mrs. Delaney.

I frowned. I didn't know what down in the mouth *meant, but Mrs. Delaney was still talking. It would have been rude to interrupt her, so I waited.*

Lark and Connor thought *down in the mouth* had to do with baking, but it is just another way for someone to say they feel very sad. When Sophie's dessert was destroyed, Sophie was down in the mouth with sadness.

Award-winning author **NATASHA DEEN** graduated from the University of Alberta with a BA in psychology. In addition to her work as a presenter and workshop facilitator with schools, she writes for kids, young adults and adults. Natasha was the 2013 Regional Writer in Residence for the Metro Edmonton Library Federation. Natasha lives in Edmonton, Alberta. For more information, please visit her website at natashadeen.com.

DON'T MISS THE REST of the LARK BA the DETECTIVE SERIES

"A problem-solving adventure led by a lovable character."

—*SCHOOL LIBRARY JOURNAL*

"Lark's sparkly presence on the chapter-book shelves will be welcomed by many."

—*KIRKUS REVIEWS*

LARK
TAKES A BOW

Illustrated by
MARCUS CUTLER

NATASHA
DEEN

orca Echoes

"Lark's authentic
success at sleuthing
ensures her a place at
the chapter-book table."

—*KIRKUS REVIEWS*

orca Echoes